THE LODGE

A Thrilling Crime Mystery

ARIEL SANDERS

Copyright © 2025 by ARIEL SANDERS
All rights reserved.

No part of this book may be reproduced, stored in a retrieval system, or transmitted in any form or by any means—electronic, mechanical, photocopying, recording, or otherwise—without the prior written permission of the publisher, except in the case of brief quotations used in reviews.

This book is intended for entertainment purposes only. While every effort has been made to ensure accuracy, the author and publisher make no representations or warranties regarding the completeness, accuracy, or reliability of the information contained within. The reader assumes full responsibility for their interpretation and application of any content in this book.

Index

Chapter 1 Arrival	5
Chapter 2 Whispers in the Walls	13
Chapter 3 Hidden Architecture	28
Chapter 4 The Disappeared	35
Chapter 5 The Basement	39
Chapter 6 The Guestbook of the Dead	43
Chapter 7 Cat and Mouse	47
Chapter 8 The Fire and the Flood	52
Chapter 9 Aftermath	57
Chapter 10 Legacy of the Lodge	63

SPECIAL BONUS

Want this Bonus Ebook for *free*?

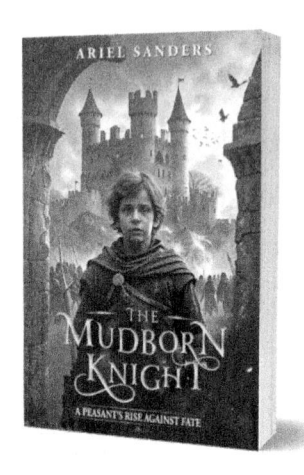

SCAN W/ YOUR CAMERA TO DOWNLOAD THE EBOOK!

SCAN ME

Chapter 1
Arrival

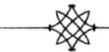

---※---

The road twisted through the mountains like a serpent, each bend revealing another stretch of asphalt that disappeared into the mist. Emma Wright stared out the passenger window, her artist's eye drawn to the way the fog wrapped around the ancient pines. There was something both beautiful and unsettling about it—the way the world seemed to end just beyond the reach of their headlights.

"How much farther?" she asked, turning to her husband.

Mark Wright kept his eyes fixed on the road, his knuckles white against the steering wheel. "GPS says another twenty minutes. Though I'm not sure how reliable that is out here." He gestured vaguely at the wilderness surrounding them.

Emma nodded, returning her gaze to the window. They had been driving for hours, leaving behind the comforts of the city for what Mark had described as a "digital detox"—a week at a remote mountain lodge with no cell service and limited internet. As a software developer constantly bombarded with notifications and deadlines, Mark had been desperate for escape. Emma had agreed, thinking the isolation might inspire her art.

Now, as they climbed higher into the mountains, a sense of unease settled in her stomach.

"There," Mark said suddenly, pointing through the windshield. "I think that's it."

The road curved once more, and Holmes Lodge emerged from the mist like a specter. It was a sprawling Victorian structure with a steep roof and ornate woodwork—beautiful in an antique way, yet somehow wrong, as if the proportions had been subtly altered. Warm light spilled from the windows, incongruous against the darkening sky.

Mark pulled into the gravel driveway, the tires crunching beneath them. "Looks cozy," he said with forced cheer, but Emma caught the slight furrow of his brow.

They sat in silence for a moment, taking in their home for the next week. The lodge was impressive—three stories of dark wood and stone, with a wide porch wrapping around the front. Yet despite its grandeur, it seemed... quiet. Too quiet.

"No other cars," Emma observed.

"It's the off-season," Mark reminded her. "Plus, the website mentioned that they never book more than a few guests at once. Exclusive experience and all that."

Emma nodded, but something about the emptiness of the parking area made her feel exposed. Before she could voice her concerns, the front door of the lodge swung open.

A tall, slender man stepped onto the porch. Even from a distance, there was something striking about him—not handsome, exactly, but memorable. His posture was impeccable, his movements deliberate as he descended the steps to meet them.

"That must be Mr. Holmes," Mark said, opening his door. "The owner."

They exited the car, and Emma shivered as the mountain air hit her skin. It wasn't just the cold that gave her goosebumps.

"Mr. and Mrs. Wright," the man called, his voice carrying easily across the driveway. "Welcome to Holmes Lodge."

Up close, Mr. Holmes was even more peculiar. His face was angular with high cheekbones and deep-set eyes, and though he smiled warmly, the expression never quite reached those eyes. They remained calculating, assessing.

"I'm Stanley Holmes," he said, extending a hand that was oddly cool and dry. "It's a pleasure to have you with us."

"Thanks for having us," Mark replied, shaking his hand. "The drive up was something else."

"Indeed. The mountains can be... protective of their secrets." Mr. Holmes's gaze shifted to Emma, and she felt a chill that had nothing to do with the temperature. "Mrs. Wright, I hope you'll find inspiration here. Mark mentioned you're an artist."

Emma forced a smile. "Yes, I am. And please, call me Emma."

"Emma," Mr. Holmes repeated, as if tasting the name. "Lovely. Well, shall we get you settled? The evening grows dark, and dinner will be served shortly."

He gestured for them to follow, and Mark moved to retrieve their luggage from the trunk. Emma hung back, her eyes drawn to the tree line beyond the lodge. For a moment, she thought she saw movement among the pines—a flash of pale skin, quickly gone.

"Emma?" Mark called, struggling with their bags. "A little help?"

She blinked, and whatever she'd seen—if she'd seen anything at all—was gone.

"Coming," she said, hurrying to assist him.

They followed Mr. Holmes into the lodge. The interior was as impressive as the exterior—high ceilings, hardwood floors, a massive stone fireplace dominating one wall of the entrance hall.

Antique furniture was arranged tastefully throughout, and the walls were adorned with landscapes in heavy gilt frames.

"This is beautiful," Emma said honestly.

"Thank you." Mr. Holmes beamed, though his eyes remained cold. "The lodge has been in my family for generations. I've dedicated my life to preserving its... unique character."

He led them up a creaking staircase to the second floor, down a long hallway lined with closed doors. The carpet runner muffled their footsteps, creating the unsettling impression that they were floating rather than walking.

"Here we are," Mr. Holmes said, stopping before the last door on the right. He produced an ornate brass key from his pocket. "Your suite."

The room beyond was spacious and well-appointed, with a four-poster bed, a sitting area near a small fireplace, and large windows overlooking the forest. A door in one wall presumably led to a bathroom.

"Dinner is served at seven in the dining room downstairs," Mr. Holmes informed them. "I hope you'll join me. It's rare that I have such... interesting company."

"We'll be there," Mark assured him.

Mr. Holmes nodded, his gaze lingering on Emma a beat too long before he turned to leave. "Rest well," he said from the doorway. "The mountain air often affects newcomers... most peculiarly."

When the door closed behind him, Emma released a breath she hadn't realized she was holding.

"Well, he's... intense," Mark said, dropping their bags onto a luggage rack.

"That's one word for it." Emma wandered to the window, looking out at the darkening forest. "This place is strange, Mark. It feels... I don't know, wrong somehow."

Mark crossed the room to stand behind her, wrapping his arms around her waist. "It's just old and remote. And Mr. Holmes is probably lonely up here by himself." He kissed the top of her head. "Relax. This is supposed to be a vacation, remember?"

Emma leaned back against him, trying to find comfort in his solidity. "I know. I'm being silly."

But as she stared out at the forest, she couldn't shake the feeling that somewhere in those dark woods, someone—or something—was staring back.

Dinner was a strangely formal affair, considering there were only three of them. The dining room was cavernous, with a table that could seat twenty but was set for just three at one end. Candles provided most of the light, their flames reflected in the darkened windows that lined one wall.

Mr. Holmes proved to be a gracious host, if somewhat peculiar in his mannerisms. He served a remarkably sophisticated meal—roasted game hen with wild mushrooms, vegetables that he claimed were foraged from the surrounding forest, and a rich, earthy wine that he poured generously into Mark's glass.

"You're not drinking, Emma?" he asked when she covered her glass with her hand.

"I've got a bit of a headache," she lied. "Probably the altitude."

Mr. Holmes studied her for a moment, then nodded. "Of course. The mountains affect different people in different ways." He turned to Mark. "But you must try this vintage. It's... quite special."

Mark, never one to refuse good wine, accepted another pour. "This is excellent," he said after a sip. "I don't think I've ever had anything quite like it."

"It's unique to this region," Mr. Holmes explained. "An old family recipe, you might say."

As dinner progressed, Emma noticed Mark becoming increasingly relaxed, his eyelids growing heavy. Mr. Holmes, on the other hand, remained perfectly composed, his movements precise, his attention fixed primarily on Emma.

"So tell me," he said as he served a dark, rich dessert, "what brings you to my humble lodge? Mark mentioned a desire to disconnect, but surely there are less... remote places to do so."

"It was the website," Mark said, his words slightly slurred. "The photographs were incredible. And the reviews..."

"Yes, our guests are often quite... effusive in their praise," Mr. Holmes said, the corner of his mouth twitching. "Though few stay in touch after leaving us."

There was something in the way he said it that made Emma's skin crawl.

"I imagine you've hosted many interesting guests over the years," she said carefully.

Mr. Holmes's eyes gleamed in the candlelight. "Oh yes. Many have passed through these doors." He gestured with his wine glass. "Some leave more of an impression than others, of course."

By the time dessert was finished, Mark was practically nodding off at the table.

"You'll sleep like the dead tonight," Mr. Holmes said, rising from his seat. "The mountain air, combined with the journey and the wine... quite soporific."

Emma helped Mark to his feet, alarmed at how unsteady he was. "I should get him upstairs."

"Of course." Mr. Holmes watched them with that same cold assessment in his eyes. "Sleep well, Emma Wright. We'll speak more tomorrow, I'm sure."

Mark was asleep almost before his head hit the pillow. Emma sat beside him on the bed, watching his chest rise and fall. His breathing seemed normal, but his face was flushed, and when she touched his forehead, he felt warm.

"Mark," she whispered, shaking him gently. "Mark, wake up."

He mumbled something incoherent and turned away from her.

Emma sighed and rose from the bed. It was just the wine, she told herself. Just the wine and the travel and the altitude. Nothing sinister about it.

But as she prepared for bed, she couldn't shake the feeling that something was very wrong with Holmes Lodge. The silence was too complete, the darkness outside their windows too absolute. And beneath it all, a sense of being watched that made her skin prickle.

It was just her imagination, she decided as she slipped into bed beside Mark's unconscious form. Just the unfamiliar surroundings playing tricks on her mind.

But as she drifted toward sleep, she could have sworn she heard something—a soft whisper, like voices carried on the wind, emanating from the vent near the ceiling.

Welcome, the voices seemed to say. Welcome home.

Chapter 2
Whispers in the Walls

Emma woke with a start, her heart pounding in her chest. The room was pitch black, the kind of darkness that exists only in places far from city lights. For a moment, she didn't remember where she was—and then it all came flooding back. Holmes Lodge. The strange Mr. Holmes. Mark's unusual drowsiness at dinner.

Mark. She reached out across the bed, her hand finding nothing but cool sheets. She sat up, squinting into the darkness.

"Mark?" she called, her voice unnaturally loud in the silent room.

No response.

She fumbled for her phone on the nightstand, using its light to illuminate the room. The bed beside her was empty, the covers thrown back. The door to the bathroom was open, revealing darkness beyond.

"Mark?" she called again, louder this time.

A floorboard creaked somewhere in the hallway outside their room. Then another. Soft, measured footsteps, moving away from their door.

Emma slipped out of bed, the wooden floor cold beneath her bare feet. She moved to the door, pressing her ear against it. The footsteps continued, growing fainter, followed by what sounded like a door opening and closing.

She turned the handle as quietly as she could and peered out into the hallway. It was empty, the runner carpet stretching into darkness in both directions. A sliver of moonlight spilled through a window at the far end, casting long shadows.

"Mark?" she whispered.

Something moved at the edge of her vision—a shadow passing across the moonlight. Emma froze, straining to see through the darkness. Was that a figure at the end of the hall? Or just her imagination distorting the shadows?

She was about to step into the hallway when another sound stopped her—voices, too faint to make out words, coming from somewhere below. She hesitated, torn between investigating and returning to the safety of their room.

The decision was made for her when she heard a familiar laugh—Mark's, followed by the deeper tones of what could only be Mr. Holmes. They were downstairs, talking. Mark had probably just gone to the bathroom and somehow ended up in conversation with their host.

Relief washed over her, followed immediately by annoyance. What was Mark thinking, wandering around in the middle of the night?

She closed the door and returned to bed, though sleep eluded her now. She lay awake, listening to the old lodge settle around her. The wind picked up outside, whistling through the eaves, creating odd harmonics that almost sounded like distant cries.

Eventually, she heard the door open, and Mark's silhouette appeared.

"Where were you?" she asked, sitting up.

Mark jumped, clearly not expecting her to be awake. "Jesus, Emma, you scared me."

"I heard you talking with Mr. Holmes."

Mark approached the bed, his movements uncertain in the darkness. "What? No, I was just in the bathroom."

"The bathroom's empty. I checked."

He sat heavily on the edge of the bed. "I mean the one downstairs. The one up here was... occupied."

"Occupied? By who? We're the only guests."

"I don't know. The door was locked. I heard water running." He shrugged. "Old houses, old plumbing. Probably just air in the pipes."

Emma frowned. Something about his explanation didn't ring true, but she was too tired to press the issue. "Come to bed," she said instead. "It's freezing."

Mark slid under the covers beside her, and she curled against him, seeking his warmth. But as she drifted back toward sleep, she couldn't shake the feeling that something wasn't right. Mark's skin felt different somehow—cooler, drier. And beneath the familiar scent of his soap, there was something else... something earthy and ancient.

She dreamed of corridors that night—endless hallways lined with doors, each one locked, each one hiding something she desperately needed to find.

Morning brought no clarity. Emma woke to find Mark already out of bed, standing at the window with a cup of coffee, staring out at the forest.

"Morning," he said without turning. "Sleep well?"

"Not really." Emma sat up, running a hand through her tangled hair. "Did you?"

"Like a log." Now he did turn, and Emma was struck by how... normal he looked. The flush from the previous night was gone, and his eyes were clear. "Mr. Holmes left coffee outside our door. Said breakfast is whenever we make it downstairs."

Emma nodded, trying to reconcile the strange events of the night with the mundane morning. Perhaps she had dreamed it all—the footsteps, the voices, Mark's mysterious absence.

After dressing, they made their way downstairs. The dining room was empty, but the table was set with pastries, fruit, and a pot of fresh coffee. There was no sign of Mr. Holmes.

"Should we wait for him?" Emma asked, taking a seat.

"He left a note saying to start without him," Mark replied, gesturing to a folded card beside the coffee pot. "Apparently he has some business to attend to this morning."

Emma picked up the card. Sure enough, it contained a brief message in an elegant, flowing script:

Please enjoy breakfast at your leisure. I've been called away on business but will return before dinner. The lodge is yours to explore—though mind the west wing, which is undergoing renovations. —S.H.

"West wing?" Emma looked up at Mark. "This place is bigger than I thought."

Mark shrugged, helping himself to a croissant. "It's an old building. Probably been added onto over the years."

They ate in silence, the enormity of the empty dining room making conversation feel somehow inappropriate. Afterward, Mark announced his intention to do some work on his laptop in their room.

"So much for a digital detox," Emma teased.

"Just for an hour or two," he promised. "Why don't you explore? Get some sketches of the place. I know that look in your eye—you're itching to draw something."

He wasn't wrong. Despite her misgivings about Holmes Lodge, there was something compelling about its architecture, its atmosphere. Her fingers did itch for a pencil.

"Alright," she agreed. "I'll scout locations. But then we're going for a walk outside. I need fresh air."

Mark kissed her cheek. "Deal."

With her sketchbook and pencils in hand, Emma set out to explore the lodge. The morning light revealed details she'd missed the previous evening—intricate woodwork along the staircase, stained glass insets in some of the windows, curious symbols carved subtly into doorframes.

She wandered through what appeared to be a library, its walls lined with leather-bound volumes, their spines unmarked. A sitting room followed, furnished with Victorian pieces that looked both elegant and uncomfortable. A conservatory with dead plants in ornate pots, the glass panels streaked with grime.

Throughout her exploration, she had the distinct feeling of being watched. Occasionally, she would turn quickly, certain she would catch someone standing behind her—but there was never anyone there.

On the ground floor, at the far end of a long corridor, she found a locked door—presumably the entrance to the "west wing" Mr. Holmes had mentioned in his note. Curious, she pressed her ear against it but heard nothing. She tried the handle, unsurprised to find it wouldn't turn.

As she was about to move away, something caught her eye—a thin line of red at the base of the door, as if someone had spilled paint on the other side. She knelt down, touching it with her fingertip. It was still wet, and when she brought her finger closer, she saw that it wasn't paint at all.

It was blood.

Emma's heart pounded as she wiped her finger on her jeans, backing away from the door. It could be innocent, she told herself. Maybe Mr. Holmes had cut himself while working. Maybe it was red wine, not blood at all.

But deep down, she knew better.

She hurried back toward the main part of the lodge, her sketchbook forgotten in her hand. As she passed a vent in the wall, she heard it again—that whispering sound, like distant voices carried on a breeze. She stopped, leaning closer to the grate.

"...another one..." the voice whispered, barely audible. "...perfect specimen..."

"...the woman suspects..." came another voice, higher-pitched.

"...no matter... she'll join him soon enough..."

Emma stumbled back from the vent, her blood running cold. She had to find Mark. They had to leave this place.

She raced up the stairs, taking them two at a time, and burst into their room without knocking. Mark was seated at the small desk, his laptop open before him.

"We need to leave," she said without preamble. "Now."

Mark turned, his expression confused. "What? Why?"

"This place is wrong," Emma said, struggling to keep her voice steady. "I heard voices in the walls, talking about us. And there's blood coming from under the door to the west wing."

Mark's face softened in a way that made Emma's stomach twist. It was the look he gave her when he thought she was being irrational. "Emma, honey, you're imagining things."

"I'm not," she insisted. "I know what I saw, what I heard."

Mark sighed, closing his laptop. "Old houses make noises. Pipes knock, wind whistles through cracks. As for the 'blood,' it was probably rust from a pipe or something."

"It wasn't rust, Mark. It was fresh. It was wet."

He stood, crossing to where she stood trembling by the door. "Emma, listen to yourself. You think our host is, what, a murderer? And he's discussing his plans through the heating vents?"

Put that way, it did sound absurd. But Emma couldn't shake the certainty of what she'd experienced. "I know how it sounds, but—"

"But nothing," Mark cut her off, his tone uncharacteristically firm. "You're stressed from work, from the drive up here. You're in an unfamiliar place with an admittedly strange host. Your imagination is running away with you."

"Mark—"

"No." He gripped her shoulders, looking directly into her eyes. "We are not leaving. We paid for a week, and I need this break. If you're really uncomfortable, we can leave in the morning. But let's at least give it one more night."

Emma wanted to argue, to insist, but the set of Mark's jaw told her it would be futile. And maybe, just maybe, he was right. Maybe she was overreacting.

"Fine," she conceded. "One more night."

"Thank you." Mark's expression softened, and he pulled her into an embrace that should have been comforting but somehow wasn't. "How about that walk? Some fresh air might help clear your head."

Emma nodded against his chest, though she was no longer sure that anywhere in or around Holmes Lodge could be considered "fresh."

They spent the afternoon exploring the grounds, keeping to the areas near the lodge. The forest was beautiful in a melancholy way—old-growth pines stretching toward a sky that remained stubbornly overcast, a carpet of needles muffling their footsteps. The air was cool and moist, carrying the scent of decomposing vegetation.

At one point, as they followed a narrow path through the trees, Emma had that feeling again—of being watched. She turned quickly, scanning the forest behind them.

And there, between two distant pines, she saw it—a figure, pale and still, watching them. It was too far away to make out details, but Emma was certain it was a person.

"Mark," she whispered, clutching his arm. "Look. Over there."

Mark followed her gaze, squinting into the distance. "I don't see anything."

"Between those two tall pines. Someone's watching us."

Mark stared a moment longer, then shook his head. "There's nothing there, Emma."

But there was. Even as Mark denied it, Emma could see the figure clearly—unmoving, unblinking, its gaze fixed on them with terrible intensity.

Then, without warning, it was gone—not ducking behind a tree or turning away, but simply... gone, as if it had never been there at all.

Emma clung to Mark's arm the rest of the walk, her eyes constantly scanning the trees around them. She saw nothing more, but the feeling of being observed never left her.

They returned to the lodge as dusk was falling, the forest behind them darkening rapidly. Mr. Holmes was waiting for them in the entrance hall, his tall figure silhouetted against the warm light of the interior.

"Ah, the Wrights," he said with that same not-quite-genuine smile. "I trust you found the grounds to your liking?"

"They're beautiful," Mark replied before Emma could speak. "You have a remarkable property here."

"Thank you. It's been in the family for... a very long time." Mr. Holmes's gaze shifted to Emma. "And you, Mrs. Wright? Did you find inspiration for your art?"

Emma forced a smile. "It's certainly a unique place."

"Indeed it is." Mr. Holmes regarded her for a moment longer, then gestured toward the dining room. "Dinner will be served shortly. Perhaps some wine first?"

"That sounds perfect," Mark said.

"Actually," Emma interjected, "I'm feeling a bit tired. I might skip dinner and turn in early."

Both men turned to look at her with eerily similar expressions of disappointment.

"Are you sure?" Mark asked. "You barely ate at breakfast."

"I can have something brought up to your room," Mr. Holmes offered, that cold assessment back in his eyes.

"No, thank you. I'm really not hungry." Emma squeezed Mark's hand. "You enjoy dinner. I'm just going to take a hot bath and go to bed."

Mark looked like he wanted to argue but eventually nodded. "Alright. I won't be late."

Mr. Holmes's expression was unreadable as he watched their exchange. "As you wish, Mrs. Wright. Rest well."

Emma climbed the stairs alone, feeling their eyes on her back until she turned the corner. In their room, she locked the door behind her, then dragged a chair over and wedged it under the handle for good measure. Only then did she allow herself to breathe.

Something was very wrong at Holmes Lodge. Wrong with Mr. Holmes, wrong with the whispering voices, wrong with Mark's dismissive attitude toward her concerns. It all felt... orchestrated somehow, as if she were moving through a play where everyone knew their lines except her.

She ran a bath as promised, hoping the hot water might ease the tension that had taken up residence between her shoulder blades. As the tub filled, she examined the bathroom more carefully than she had the previous night.

It was old-fashioned but well-maintained, with black and white tile floors, a claw-foot tub, and a pedestal sink. A large mirror hung above the sink, its frame ornate and tarnished with age.

Emma stared at her reflection, noting the dark circles under her eyes, the pallor of her skin. She looked ill, or afraid, or both.

Behind her, steam rose from the filling tub, gradually fogging the lower portion of the mirror. As she watched, something strange happened—a section of the fog cleared, as if someone had drawn a finger through it. A line appeared, then another, forming letters:

HELP

Emma spun around, her heart hammering. The bathroom was empty. She turned back to the mirror, but the word was gone, the fog once again uniform across the glass.

Had she imagined it? Was she truly losing her mind?

She shut off the water and sat on the edge of the tub, taking deep, steadying breaths. When she felt calmer, she undressed and slipped into the bath, allowing the heat to seep into her tense muscles.

She must have dozed off, because the next thing she knew, she was jerking awake at the sound of a creak. The bathwater had cooled, and the room was dark except for the sliver of light coming from the bedroom.

Another creak, and then a movement caught her eye—the mirror was moving, swinging outward from the wall like a door.

Emma sat frozen in the tub, unable to make a sound as the mirror opened just a few inches, revealing darkness beyond. For a long, terrible moment, nothing happened.

Then, slowly, fingers appeared at the edge of the opening—long, pale fingers, unnaturally thin, edging around the frame of the mirror.

Emma's paralysis broke. She surged from the tub, water cascading around her as she grabbed a towel and backed toward the door to the bedroom, her eyes fixed on those ghostly fingers.

Before she could scream, the fingers withdrew, and the mirror swung closed with a soft click. The bathroom was normal again, as if nothing had happened.

Emma backed into the bedroom, fumbling for her clothes with shaking hands. She had to leave. Now. With or without Mark.

She had just finished dressing when she heard footsteps in the hallway outside—the measured tread that could only belong to Mr. Holmes, followed by Mark's lighter step. They were talking, their voices too low to make out words.

Emma moved to the door, pressing her ear against it. They had stopped just outside, their conversation becoming clearer.

"...really appreciate this," Mark was saying, his words slightly slurred again. "She's been so stressed lately. Imagining things."

"It's not uncommon," came Mr. Holmes's smooth reply. "The mind can play curious tricks, especially in places with such... history as this lodge."

"Still, I'm sorry about her behavior today. The accusations..."

"Think nothing of it. The important thing is that you're enjoying your stay."

"I am. Very much so. This wine is incredible."

"It's a special reserve. Not everyone appreciates its... unique qualities."

Their voices moved away down the hall, and Emma stepped back from the door, her mind racing. Mark was apologizing for her behavior? Discussing her with Mr. Holmes as if she were a troublesome child?

She returned to the bathroom, approaching the mirror with caution. Examining it closely, she could see what she'd missed before—a thin seam where the frame met the wall, almost invisible unless you knew to look for it.

A panel behind the mirror. A secret passage of some kind.

She placed her fingers at the edge and pulled gently. The mirror swung outward silently, revealing a dark, narrow corridor beyond. Cold air rushed out, carrying a smell of damp stone and something else—something metallic and organic that made her stomach turn.

Emma let the mirror swing closed, backing away. She didn't need to explore that passage to know where it led—to the west wing, to the source of those whispering voices, to whatever dark secret lay at the heart of Holmes Lodge.

She returned to the bedroom and waited, seated in the chair by the door, for Mark to return. It was well past midnight when he finally did, fumbling with the locked door before she opened it.

"Emma," he slurred, blinking at her silhouette in the darkness. "Why're you still up?"

"We need to talk, Mark." She closed the door behind him, keeping her distance.

"Can't it wait till morning?" He stumbled toward the bed, collapsing onto it fully clothed. "I'm beat."

"There's a secret passage behind our bathroom mirror."

Mark groaned, rolling onto his back. "Not this again, Emma. Please."

"I saw it, Mark. It opens into a passage. And there's something wrong with this place, with Mr. Holmes. The way you're acting... it's like you've been drugged or something."

Mark's laugh was hollow. "The only thing I've had is some excellent wine. And maybe that's what you need—something to help you relax."

"I don't need to relax. I need you to listen to me." Emma's voice rose despite her efforts to keep it steady. "Someone wrote 'HELP' on our bathroom mirror. There's blood under the door to the west wing. There are secret passages in the walls. And you're acting like none of this is concerning."

Mark sat up, his expression darkening. "Because it isn't, Emma. The writing was probably just condensation. The 'blood' is rust or paint. And old houses have all sorts of strange architectural features."

"Why are you defending this place? Why can't you see what's happening?"

"Because nothing is happening!" Now Mark was shouting. "Nothing except you having some kind of breakdown. First it was the voices in the vents, then figures in the woods, now secret passages? Do you hear yourself?"

Emma stared at him, struck by the vehemence in his voice. This wasn't like Mark—Mark, who was always calm, always rational, always willing to hear her out even when he disagreed.

"You're not yourself," she said quietly. "Ever since we arrived, you've been different. The wine—"

"Enough about the damn wine!" Mark stood, swaying slightly. "I'm going to sleep. In the morning, you're either going to drop this nonsense, or I'm calling Dr. Reeves to adjust your medication."

Emma felt as if she'd been slapped. "My medication? I haven't been on anxiety meds for over a year."

"Maybe that's the problem." Mark's voice was cold, dismissive. "Maybe you should be."

He turned away from her, collapsing back onto the bed and rolling to face the wall. Within minutes, his breathing had deepened into sleep, leaving Emma standing alone in the darkened room.

She didn't sleep that night. Instead, she sat in the chair by the window, watching the forest beyond, where shadows moved among the trees that had nothing to do with the wind. And all the while, from somewhere deep within the walls of Holmes Lodge, she could hear them—soft, persistent whispers, calling her name.

Chapter 3
Hidden Architecture

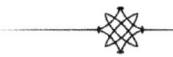

Morning brought a tension between them that was palpable. Mark was quiet as he dressed, avoiding Emma's gaze. For her part, Emma watched him with wary eyes, looking for signs of whatever influence Holmes Lodge—or its master—had exerted over him.

"I'm sorry about last night," Mark said finally, breaking the silence. "I shouldn't have shouted."

"No, you shouldn't have," Emma agreed, too tired for pretense. "And you shouldn't have discussed me with Mr. Holmes as if I were having a mental breakdown."

Mark had the grace to look ashamed. "You heard that?"

"I heard enough."

He sighed, running a hand through his hair. "Look, I am worried about you. You're seeing threats where there aren't any. It's not healthy."

"What's not healthy is dismissing what I've experienced," Emma countered. "The mirror does open, Mark. There is a passage behind it. I can show you."

Mark held up a hand. "Let's just... take it easy today, alright? No talk of secret passages or mysterious figures. Let's just try to enjoy our vacation."

It was a cease-fire, not a resolution, but Emma was too exhausted to argue further. "Fine."

They went down to breakfast together, the silence between them stretching thin. There was no sign of Mr. Holmes, but the table was set as it had been the previous day, with fresh pastries and coffee. Another note card sat beside the coffee pot.

Mark read it aloud: "*Please enjoy your day. I've been called away on business again but will return for dinner. Feel free to explore the lodge and grounds, though I must insist once more that the west wing remains off-limits for your safety. —S.H.*"

"Convenient how he's never around during the day," Emma remarked.

Mark gave her a warning look. "Emma..."

"I'm just saying it's odd, that's all."

They ate in silence, the weight of their argument hanging between them. Afterward, Mark announced his intention to do some more work on his laptop. "The WiFi is surprisingly good here," he said, settling in the common room with his computer. "I might as well catch up on some emails while we're here."

Emma nodded, knowing this was his way of creating space between them after their argument. "I think I'll explore a bit more," she said. "Maybe take some photos of the lodge. The architecture is... interesting."

Mark barely looked up from his screen. "Just stay out of the west wing like Holmes asked, okay?"

"I'm not a child, Mark," she replied, the irritation clear in her voice as she left the room.

Emma wandered the main hallway, studying the ornate woodwork and peculiar layout of the lodge. Something about it felt wrong—rooms that should connect didn't, hallways that seemed longer inside than they appeared from outside. As an artist, she had an eye for spatial relationships, and Holmes Lodge defied conventional geometry.

In a small study off the main corridor, she found a desk with several drawers. Most were empty or contained tourist brochures and maps, but in the back of the bottom drawer, hidden beneath a stack of old newspapers, Emma's fingers brushed against a rolled tube of paper.

She carefully extracted it—an architectural blueprint, yellowed with age. Unrolling it on the desk, her breath caught. It was a floor plan of Holmes Lodge, but not as she knew it. This design showed a much larger structure, with extensive wings on either side and—her heart raced—a complex network of narrow passages labeled "servant tunnels" running between the walls.

Most disturbing was the clear indication of a "subterranean level" beneath the main floor, accessible by several hidden staircases. One of those access points was marked in a location very near their bathroom.

Emma took photos of the blueprint with her phone before carefully returning it to its hiding place. When she returned to Mark, she found him still absorbed in his work.

"Mark, I need to show you something," she said, sitting beside him and opening the photos on her phone.

He glanced at the screen, brow furrowing. "What am I looking at?"

"Floor plans. Original blueprints for this place." She zoomed in on the section showing their room and the hidden passage. "See this? There are tunnels in the walls, Mark. And look—" she pointed to their bathroom, "—there's an entrance right where I saw the mirror move."

Mark sighed, pushing her phone away. "Emma, old houses like this often had service corridors. It doesn't mean anything sinister."

"But don't you think it's strange that Mr. Holmes never mentioned them? That he specifically keeps us away from certain areas?" Her voice rose with frustration. "There's an entire underground level that shouldn't exist!"

"What shouldn't exist is this paranoia," Mark snapped, then immediately looked regretful. "I'm sorry, that was harsh. But these are just old blueprints. The lodge was probably renovated since then. Most of those passages are probably sealed up now."

Emma stood, tucking her phone away. "I know what I saw, Mark. And I'm going to prove it to you."

The rest of the day passed in uneasy tension. They ate lunch separately, and Emma spent the afternoon sketching the exterior of the lodge, noting discrepancies between what she could see and what the blueprints had shown. The building's footprint seemed too small for the extensive layout in the plans.

Dinner with Mr. Holmes was another uncomfortable affair. He served them a hearty stew, his manner as politely unsettling as ever.

"I trust you've been enjoying your stay?" he asked, filling their wine glasses.

"It's been enlightening," Emma replied, watching as Mark drank deeply from his glass.

"The lodge has many stories to tell, for those who listen," Mr. Holmes said with a thin smile. "Though not all tales are meant for every ear."

After dinner, they retired to their room, Mark oddly lethargic. "I'm exhausted," he mumbled, struggling to keep his eyes open. "Must be the wine."

"You'll sleep like the dead tonight," Emma repeated Mr. Holmes's earlier words, helping Mark to bed.

He was asleep within minutes, his breathing deep and even. Emma sat in the armchair by the window, waiting. The house creaked and settled around her as the night deepened. She checked her watch: 1:17 AM.

That's when she heard it—a soft click from the bathroom. Heart pounding, Emma crept to the doorway. In the dim light, she watched as the mirror slowly swung outward, revealing a dark passage beyond. A pale hand gripped the edge of the mirror.

Emma backed away, stumbling to the bed. "Mark!" she hissed, shaking him. "Mark, wake up!" But he remained unresponsive, drugged into a deep sleep.

The mirror stopped moving. Emma held her breath. After a long moment, it slowly closed again with a soft click.

She spent the rest of the night in the chair, a heavy lamp clutched in her hands, watching the bathroom door. When morning finally came, Mark awoke refreshed while Emma was hollow-eyed from her vigil.

"You look terrible," he said, concerned. "Did you sleep at all?"

"The mirror opened last night," she said flatly. "Someone was there, watching us."

Mark rubbed his face. "Emma, please. It was probably just a dream."

"I was wide awake. You were drugged."

"Drugged? That's ridiculous." He sat on the edge of the bed. "Look, the house is old. It settles, makes noises. The mirror might have shifted because the wall isn't perfectly level."

"Then explain why I can't open it," Emma challenged. "I've tried. If it's just loosely mounted, I should be able to move it too."

"You're being irrational," Mark insisted. "There's a logical explanation."

"Yes, there is," Emma said, gathering her jacket. "And I'm going to find it."

Chapter 4
The Disappeared

The morning air was crisp and cold as Emma made her way into the woods surrounding Holmes Lodge. Mark had stayed behind, claiming he needed to finish some work, but Emma suspected he just wanted distance from her "paranoia."

She followed a narrow hiking trail, snapping photos of the landscape with her camera. The fog hung between the trees like ghostly curtains, occasionally parting to reveal glimpses of the mountains beyond. It was beautiful but unsettling, as if the forest itself were hiding secrets.

After about thirty minutes of walking, Emma veered off the path, drawn to a small clearing where the ground looked recently disturbed. As she approached, her foot struck something solid beneath the leaf litter.

Kneeling, she brushed away the leaves and soil to reveal the corner of what appeared to be a suitcase. Her heart raced as she dug around it, eventually freeing a mud-covered travel bag.

Emma unzipped it with trembling fingers. Inside were clothes, a toiletry bag, and a wallet. She opened the wallet, finding a driver's license inside.

"Jennifer Reeves," she read aloud, staring at the smiling face in the photo. The license had been issued three years ago. With shaking hands, Emma took out her phone and searched the name.

The results made her blood run cold. Jennifer Reeves had been reported missing while on a hiking trip in these mountains—

almost exactly one year ago. Her rental car had been found at a trailhead, but there had been no sign of Jennifer herself.

Until now.

Emma carefully repacked everything as she had found it, her mind racing. This couldn't be a coincidence. Holmes Lodge, the hidden passages, Mr. Holmes's strange behavior, and now this—a missing woman's belongings buried in the woods.

She took photos of the suitcase and its contents before covering it again, marking the location on her phone's map. This was evidence, proof that something was very wrong here.

When Emma returned to the lodge, she found Mark in their room, looking pale and disoriented.

"Are you okay?" she asked, momentarily setting aside her discovery.

"I don't know," he admitted. "I feel strange. Lightheaded. Maybe it's the altitude."

Emma sat beside him on the bed. "Mark, I found something in the woods. Something disturbing." She showed him the photos of the suitcase and the license, then explained about Jennifer Reeves.

For once, Mark didn't immediately dismiss her. He stared at the photos, a troubled expression crossing his face. "This is... concerning," he admitted. "We should tell someone."

"Tell who? There's no cell service, no landline I can find. Holmes is our only connection to the outside world, and I think he might be involved." Emma lowered her voice. "I think we should leave. Now."

Mark nodded slowly. "Maybe you're right. Let's pack up and go after dinner. We'll tell Holmes we have an emergency back home or something."

Emma felt a flood of relief that Mark was finally taking her seriously. "Thank you," she whispered, squeezing his hand.

At dinner that evening, the tension was unbearable. Emma struggled to maintain a casual demeanor as Mr. Holmes served them a rich beef stew and fresh bread.

"You seem troubled, Ms. Emma," Holmes observed, his eyes unnervingly perceptive. "Is everything to your liking?"

"Everything's fine," Emma lied. "I'm just a bit tired from hiking today."

"Ah yes, the woods are beautiful this time of year." Holmes smiled thinly. "Did you find anything interesting out there?"

The question sent a chill down Emma's spine. "Just taking photos," she said, forcing a smile. "The light through the fog is quite atmospheric."

"Indeed. People often leave things behind in these woods," Holmes said, his gaze never leaving her face. "Nature reclaims what it can."

Under the table, Emma's hand found Mark's and squeezed it tightly. Mark cleared his throat. "Mr. Holmes, I'm afraid we'll need to cut our stay short. I've received word of a family emergency."

Mr. Holmes's expression didn't change, but something cold flickered in his eyes. "How unfortunate. When will you be departing?"

"First thing tomorrow," Mark said firmly.

"I understand. I'll prepare your bill." Holmes poured more tea for Mark. "Please, finish your meal. It may be some time before you have another home-cooked dinner."

Emma watched in horror as Mark took a long drink of his tea. She had left hers untouched, suspicion making her cautious. Throughout the remainder of the meal, she observed with growing dread as Mark's movements became sluggish, his speech slightly slurred.

Back in their room, Mark collapsed onto the bed, barely able to keep his eyes open. "Don't feel right," he mumbled. "Something's wrong."

"He drugged you," Emma said, panic rising in her throat. "Mark, you need to stay awake. We need to leave now."

But it was too late. Mark's eyes fluttered closed, his breathing becoming deep and regular. Emma shook him desperately, but he wouldn't wake.

She paced the room, terror mounting. They were trapped. Holmes had drugged Mark, knowing they planned to leave. Whatever fate had befallen Jennifer Reeves now awaited them.

Emma barricaded the door with a chair and kept watch through the night, the butterknife from dinner clutched in her hand. But nothing happened. No one tried to enter. The mirror remained closed.

When morning came, Emma awoke with a start, realizing she had dozed off despite her terror. The chair was still wedged under the doorknob, but something was wrong.

The bed was empty. Mark was gone.

Chapter 5
The Basement

Emma stared at the empty bed, her mind refusing to process what she was seeing. The sheets were rumpled where Mark had lain, but there was no sign of him. The chair was still wedged beneath the doorknob, undisturbed.

"Mark?" she called, her voice thin with panic. She checked the bathroom—empty. The mirror remained firmly in place when she tugged at it, refusing to reveal its secrets.

How had they taken him? The window was locked from the inside, and the door hadn't been forced. It was as if he had simply vanished.

With trembling hands, Emma gathered her essentials—phone, wallet, the small knife she'd kept from dinner—and stuffed them into her pockets. She removed the chair and cautiously opened the door, peering into the empty hallway.

The lodge was eerily silent as she made her way downstairs. In the dining room, she found a place set for one, with fresh coffee and pastries. Another note card sat beside the plate: *"Good morning, Emma. Mark mentioned he needed to head into town early. I've prepared breakfast for you. —S.H."*

"Liar," Emma whispered, crumpling the note in her fist.

She heard movement from the kitchen and steeled herself to confront Mr. Holmes, but when she pushed open the door, the room was empty. A pot of coffee still warm on the stove, but no sign of anyone.

"Mr. Holmes?" she called out, trying to keep her voice steady. "Where's Mark?"

No answer came. Emma moved through the house methodically, checking each room, finding nothing but emptiness and silence. When she tried the front door, she found it unlocked.

Outside, rain poured down in sheets, turning the driveway into a river of mud. Their car sat where they had parked it, but a quick check revealed the engine wouldn't start—the battery cables had been disconnected.

"Damn it," she muttered, slamming the hood closed. The storm was too severe to attempt walking out. She was trapped, just as Holmes had planned.

Back inside, Emma's panic gave way to cold determination. Mark was somewhere in this house, and she would find him.

She returned to the study where she'd found the blueprints, retrieving them from their hiding place. According to the plans, there were multiple access points to the lower levels—one in the kitchen pantry, another behind a bookcase in the library, and a third near the back stairwell.

As Emma studied the plans, a faint sound reached her ears—a low moan, almost inaudible beneath the storm's rumble. She froze, listening intently. There it was again, coming from below. A human sound, filled with pain.

"Mark," she breathed, following the sound to a small library off the main hall.

The room was lined with bookshelves, dusty volumes filling every space. According to the blueprint, there should be an entrance here, behind one of these shelves. Emma ran her hands along the woodwork, searching for a mechanism, a switch, anything.

As she pressed against a section of molding, she heard a click. The bookshelf to her right shifted slightly. Heart pounding, Emma pulled at the edge of the shelf, revealing darkness beyond.

A narrow staircase descended into blackness. The moaning was louder now, unmistakable. Emma turned on her phone's flashlight and began her descent, each step creaking beneath her weight.

The air grew colder and damper as she descended, the smell of mold and something else—something metallic and sickeningly sweet—filling her nostrils. The stairs ended in a low-ceilinged corridor lined with pipes and electrical conduits.

Emma followed the corridor, her light casting grotesque shadows on the stone walls. The moaning had stopped, replaced by an oppressive silence broken only by the occasional drip of water.

The corridor opened into a larger space—what might once have been a wine cellar, now converted to an altogether different purpose. Emma's light revealed a nightmare.

Hooks hung from the ceiling, some bearing what looked disturbingly like human remains in various stages of decay. Steel tables lined one wall, their surfaces stained dark. Buckets of what could only be lye sat beneath them. Against another wall stood shelves of chemicals, surgical tools, and neatly labeled jars containing unidentifiable specimens.

A butchering room. A processing station for human beings.

Emma clapped a hand over her mouth to stifle her scream. She swept her light across the room, searching desperately for Mark among the hanging forms, praying she wouldn't find him there.

Instead, her beam fell upon a figure strapped to a table in the corner—alive, but unconscious. Mark's face was pale, his chest rising and falling with shallow breaths.

"Mark!" Emma rushed to him, her hands fumbling with the leather restraints around his wrists and ankles. "Mark, wake up. Please, wake up."

His eyelids fluttered but didn't open. Whatever Holmes had given him was powerful.

As Emma worked at the restraints, a soft chuckle echoed through the chamber. She whirled around, her light catching Mr. Holmes as he stepped from the shadows, a bone saw in his gloved hand.

"You weren't supposed to find this yet," he said pleasantly, as if they were discussing a surprise party. "I had plans for you both. A proper sequence. But I suppose we'll have to improvise now."

Emma backed against the table, positioning herself between Mr. Holmes and Mark. "Stay back," she warned, holding up her pathetic dinner knife.

Mr. Holmes smiled indulgently. "You have spirit, Emma. I appreciate that. The frightened ones are so disappointingly predictable."

Chapter 6
The Guestbook of the Dead

"What have you done to him?" Emma demanded, her voice steadier than she felt.

"Nothing permanent. Yet." Mr. Holmes set the bone saw on a nearby table with deliberate care. "He's merely sedated. I prefer my subjects unconscious for the initial preparation. Reduces stress hormones in the tissue."

Emma fought against the rising bile in her throat. "You're insane."

"On the contrary. I'm methodical. Precise." Holmes gestured to the room around them. "This is craftsmanship, Emma. I don't expect you to appreciate it, of course."

Emma's eyes darted around the room, searching for a weapon, an escape route, anything. Near a dark doorway, she spotted a wooden cabinet that hadn't been visible from the entrance.

"Why are you doing this?" she asked, trying to keep him talking while she inched sideways, drawing him away from Mark.

"Why does anyone perfect a craft? For the satisfaction of the work itself." Mr. Holmes followed her movement, maintaining the distance between them. "I've been refining my process for decades. The lodge provides the perfect setting—remote, private, with a steady supply of suitable materials."

"People," Emma corrected sharply. "Not materials. People."

Mr. Holmes shrugged. "Semantics. They serve a purpose in death they never could in life. Their bones become my art. Their essence feeds my garden."

Emma reached the cabinet, keeping her back to it. "And no one ever investigates? No one misses them?"

"People go missing in these mountains every year. Hikers get lost, climbers fall. Nature is dangerous." Mr. Holmes smiled thinly. "I merely... assist the process occasionally."

With a sudden movement, Emma yanked open the cabinet behind her, using it as a shield between herself and Mr. Holmes. Inside, she found a leather-bound book and stacks of photographs. She grabbed them, retreating behind the cabinet door.

"Ah, you've found my ledger," Holmes remarked, sounding more annoyed than concerned. "My record-keeping is impeccable. I document each acquisition thoroughly."

Emma flipped open the book with trembling hands. Page after page of names and dates, spanning decades. Next to each entry were clinical notes: "Processed 4/17. Bones excellent quality. Liver damaged (alcohol)." Some entries included small sketches of bone structures or notations about "specimen quality."

The most recent entry chilled her to the core: "Mark Wright. Arrival 10/23. Processing scheduled 10/26. Companion (Emma) to be processed 10/27."

"You're a monster," Emma whispered, looking up from the book to Mr. Holmes's impassive face.

"I prefer 'collector,'" he corrected. "Or 'artist,' if you're feeling generous."

Emma shuffled through the photographs—smiling couples posing outside the lodge, families on hiking trips, all oblivious to their fate. The final photo showed her and Mark on their first day, Mr. Holmes standing slightly behind them.

As she backed away, her foot struck something solid beneath a work table. Crouching down, she saw a pile of clothing—and protruding from it, a skeletal hand still clutching a familiar phone case.

Mark's phone.

Emma's stomach heaved as she realized the implications. The body on the table wasn't Mark—it was someone else Holmes had captured. And Mark...

She looked up at the hooks hanging from the ceiling, the partially decomposed remains swaying gently in the draft from the corridor.

"What did you do to him?" she demanded, her voice breaking. "Where is Mark?"

Mr. Holmes's expression remained placid. "Your companion proved unusually resistant to the sedative. I was forced to accelerate my timeline." He gestured toward one of the hanging forms. "He's there, I'm afraid. Nearly ready for the cleaning process. His bones will make a splendid addition to my collection."

Emma vomited then, her body rejecting the horror before her mind could fully process it. As she retched, Holmes approached, his footsteps unhurried.

"It's all quite distressing at first, I understand," he said soothingly. "But there's a certain beauty to it, once you accept the inevitability."

Through tears and bile, Emma saw him reaching for a syringe on the table. With desperate strength, she hurled the ledger at his face and bolted for the corridor they'd entered through.

"You can run, Emma," Holmes called after her, his voice echoing in the stone chamber. "But this is my home. I know every passage, every hiding place. And the doors are all locked."

Emma sprinted through the dark corridor, her phone's light bouncing wildly off the stone walls. Behind her, she heard Holmes's measured footsteps, unhurried and confident.

He knew she had nowhere to go.

Chapter 7
Cat and Mouse

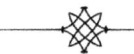

Emma's breath came in ragged gasps as she fled deeper into the tunnel network. The beam of her phone's flashlight wavered over damp stone walls, creating grotesque dancing shadows. Behind her, Holmes's footsteps echoed with unhurried confidence.

"There's no need to make this unpleasant, Emma," his voice carried through the darkness. "The tunnels can be quite disorienting. You wouldn't want to get lost down here."

She ducked into a side passage, trying to muffle her breathing. The tunnels formed a maze beneath the lodge, far more extensive than the blueprints had indicated. Some passages were narrow, forcing her to turn sideways to squeeze through, while others opened into small chambers with multiple exits.

Emma tried to maintain her sense of direction, but after several turns, she was hopelessly disoriented. The only certainty was that she needed to keep moving, to put as much distance as possible between herself and Mr. Holmes.

"I've lived with these tunnels for decades," Holmes called out, his voice seemingly coming from everywhere at once. "They speak to me. The stones themselves are my allies."

A scrabbling sound from ahead froze Emma in place. Rats. She swallowed her revulsion and pressed on.

The passage widened into a chamber that might once have been a storage room. Rotting wooden shelves lined the walls, holding dusty mason jars and rusted tools. Emma's light caught something carved into the stone wall—crude letters etched deep.

HE TAKES THE BONES

Below it, more desperate messages:

HELP US NO WAY OUT HE KNOWS THE TUNNELS

Her light revealed more carvings, dozens of them covering the walls. Pleas for help. Warnings. Names and dates going back nearly fifty years.

In one corner, huddled against the wall, was what remained of someone who had hidden here long ago—a skeleton still wearing tattered clothing, fingers worn to nubs from scratching at the unyielding stone.

Emma bit back a sob. This poor soul had died here, alone in the darkness. Just as she would, if she couldn't find a way out.

"I see you've found one of my guests," Mr. Holmes's voice came from just outside the chamber. "Not everyone appreciates my hospitality. Some try to leave prematurely."

Emma ducked behind a fallen shelf as Mr. Holmes's silhouette appeared in the doorway. He held a lantern high, its yellow light casting long shadows.

"The unfortunate woman you've discovered lasted nearly a week down here," he continued conversationally. "Most give up much sooner. They beg me to end their suffering." He sighed. "I always oblige, of course. I'm not cruel."

Emma held her breath, pressing herself against the cold stone floor. Her hand touched something metal—a rusty screwdriver, dropped by some previous victim.

"I wonder how long you'll last, Emma," Mr. Holmes mused, sweeping his lantern across the room. "You have more spirit than most. I admire that."

The light passed inches from Emma's hiding place, then moved on. Mr. Holmes lingered a moment longer before continuing down another passage. "Take your time," his voice floated back. "I'm a patient man."

When his footsteps faded, Emma crawled from her hiding place, clutching the screwdriver. Her mind raced. She couldn't defeat Holmes in direct confrontation—he was stronger, knew the terrain, and had who knew what weapons at his disposal. Her only hope was to outsmart him, to set a trap.

She explored the chamber more thoroughly, finding a collection of tools and supplies left by previous victims: rags, empty bottles, matches, a flashlight with dead batteries. In one corner, someone had attempted to dig through the mortar between stones, creating a small hollow that led nowhere.

Emma gathered what she could carry. The rusty screwdriver, a length of frayed rope, the matches, and several rags. She also found a half-empty bottle of cleaning fluid, its label long faded but the sharp chemical smell unmistakable.

Moving as quietly as possible, she backtracked to a junction she'd passed earlier, where three tunnels converged. There, she began to prepare.

She soaked the rags in the cleaning fluid, positioning them at strategic points where the stone floor met the wooden support beams. The sodden rags formed a rough circle around the junction, with one long trail leading down the passage she intended to use as her escape route.

Next, she unraveled the rope, creating a tripwire across the main tunnel entrance, tied low to the ground where it would be difficult to see in lantern light. The screwdriver she kept, her only weapon against the monster hunting her.

Emma positioned herself in an alcove near the junction, waiting in darkness. She had turned off her phone to conserve its dwindling battery, leaving only the faint glow of emergency lights far down one corridor to provide any illumination.

Time stretched endlessly in the darkness. Minutes or hours could have passed as Emma crouched, muscles cramping, ears straining for any sound. Finally, she heard what she'd been waiting for—the steady tread of Mr. Holmes's footsteps, approaching from the passage to her left.

The yellow glow of his lantern preceded him, growing brighter as he neared the junction. Emma tensed, match ready.

"I know you're near, Emma," Holmes called. "I can smell your fear."

As his silhouette appeared at the entrance to the junction, Emma held her breath. One more step...

Holmes's foot caught the tripwire. He stumbled forward, regaining his balance quickly but dropping his lantern. It rolled across the floor, miraculously remaining lit.

Now.

Emma struck the match and touched it to the nearest rag. The chemical-soaked fabric caught immediately, blue flames racing along the trail she had created. Within seconds, the junction was surrounded by fire, cutting off the tunnel behind Mr. Holmes.

Mr. Holmes's face, illuminated by the growing flames, showed surprise followed by cold fury. "Clever girl," he said, advancing toward Emma's hiding place. "But fire can be as dangerous to you as to me."

Emma bolted, racing down her planned escape route, the flames spreading behind her as they caught on ancient timbers and years of accumulated dust. Smoke began to fill the tunnels, thick and acrid.

Behind her, Mr. Holmes gave chase, no longer unhurried but moving with swift purpose. The fire was spreading faster than Emma had anticipated, consuming the old wooden supports and creating a deadly maze of flame and smoke.

She ran blindly now, eyes stinging, lungs burning. The roar of the fire drowned out all other sounds, including Mr. Holmes's pursuit. The tunnels became a hellish inferno, stone walls radiating heat, smoke filling every passage.

Emma stumbled, disoriented, her only guide the slightly fresher air coming from what she hoped was an exit. As she rounded a corner, a hand shot out from a side passage, grabbing her wrist.

Mr. Holmes's face loomed from the smoke, his pristine appearance gone. Soot streaked his features, and blood ran from a cut on his forehead. "You've destroyed everything," he snarled. "My collection. My life's work."

Emma drove the screwdriver into his shoulder with all her strength. Holmes howled, releasing her. She staggered away as the tunnel behind them collapsed in a shower of burning debris.

The last she saw of Mr. Holmes, he was disappearing into the smoke, flames catching at his clothing.

Chapter 8
The Fire and the Flood

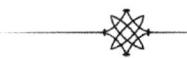

Emma crawled through the suffocating darkness, smoke burning her lungs with every breath. The fire had spread through the tunnel network with terrifying speed, feeding on decades of dry wood and dust. Behind her, the distant roar of collapsing passages urged her forward.

The tunnel sloped upward now, giving her hope. Surely this led somewhere other than deeper into Mr. Holmes's underground chamber of horrors. Her hands were raw from feeling her way along rough stone, her knees bleeding through her jeans.

A different sound reached her ears over the crackle of flames—the steady patter of rain. Fresh air brushed her face, carrying the sweet scent of pine and earth.

With renewed energy, Emma scrambled up the increasingly steep passage. The tunnel narrowed, becoming little more than a drainage pipe. She clawed at roots and earth, feeling rain on her fingers. One final push, and she emerged into the stormy night.

Emma lay on her back in the mud, letting the rain wash over her soot-streaked face. She had surfaced in the woods some distance from the lodge, which was now visible through the trees as a glowing inferno against the night sky. Flames poured from every window, illuminating the clearing in hellish orange light.

The fire had spread to the main building, just as she'd feared. Any evidence of Mr. Holmes's crimes would be destroyed, including the bodies of his victims. Including Mark.

A sob tore from Emma's throat, raw with smoke and grief. She had escaped, but at what cost? Mark was gone, and with the lodge burning to the ground, there would be little evidence of what had happened here.

Lightning split the sky, followed by a deafening crack of thunder. The storm was intensifying, rain coming down in sheets. Water ran in rivulets down the hillside, pooling around Emma as she struggled to her feet.

She needed to get away from the lodge, to find help. Stumbling through the dark forest, Emma followed the downward slope, hoping it would lead to a road or trail. The rain had turned the ground treacherous, mud sliding beneath her feet. Twice she fell, the second time tumbling down a steep embankment.

When she came to rest at the bottom, dazed and battered, Emma found herself on what appeared to be a service road. Following it blindly, she pushed forward through the deluge.

Time lost meaning as she trudged through the storm. Her soaked clothes hung heavily from her exhausted frame, her mind cycling through images of horror—Mark's phone in a skeletal hand, the carvings on the walls, Holmes's placid smile as he discussed his "craft."

A flash of light ahead caught her attention—not the orange glow of fire, but the steady beam of a flashlight. Emma tried to call out, but her smoke-damaged voice produced only a hoarse whisper. She waved her arms frantically as the light approached.

The beam caught her face, momentarily blinding her. "Hello?" a male voice called. "Is someone there?"

"Help," Emma managed to croak. "Please, help."

The beam lowered, and a figure hurried toward her—a forest ranger in a rain poncho, concern etched on his weathered face.

"Ma'am? Are you okay?" he asked, taking in her battered appearance.

Emma collapsed against him, her remaining strength evaporating. "Lodge... fire... people dead..." she gasped, before darkness claimed her.

She drifted in and out of consciousness as the ranger carried her to his vehicle. Snippets of radio communication reached her through the fog.

"...female hiker, early thirties, suffering smoke inhalation and exposure..." "...mentioned fire at Holmes Lodge..." "...requesting backup and emergency services..."

Later, the whine of an ambulance siren pierced her awareness. Hands lifted her onto a stretcher. An oxygen mask was placed over her face, blessed air flowing into her damaged lungs.

"Can you tell us your name?" a paramedic asked, his face swimming above her.

"Emma," she whispered through the mask. "Emma Wright."

"You're safe now, Emma. We're taking you to the hospital."

Safety. The concept seemed foreign after what she'd experienced. Would she ever feel safe again?

As the ambulance doors closed, Emma caught a final glimpse of the forest through the rain-streaked windows. Somewhere in that darkness, Holmes Lodge continued to burn, taking its secrets with it. But one terrible certainty remained—if Mr. Holmes had somehow survived the fire and tunnel collapse, he would never stop looking for her.

The ambulance pulled away, siren wailing into the storm-tossed night. Emma closed her eyes, surrendering to exhaustion. Her last conscious thought was of Mark, and the life they'd planned together—a life now consumed by flames and the insatiable hunger of a madman who collected human bones.

Chapter 9
Aftermath

White light assaulted Emma's eyes as she drifted back to consciousness. The antiseptic smell and rhythmic beeping of monitors told her she was in a hospital before her vision cleared enough to confirm it. An IV dripped clear fluid into her arm, and an oxygen cannula rested beneath her nose.

"She's awake," a nurse called, appearing at Emma's bedside. "Ms. Wright? Can you hear me?"

Emma tried to speak, but her throat felt raw, as if she'd swallowed broken glass. She managed a weak nod instead.

"You're at Ridgemont Memorial Hospital," the nurse explained, checking her vitals. "You've been here for three days. Your lungs were badly damaged from smoke inhalation, but you're going to recover."

Three days. The realization hit Emma with unexpected force. Three days of unconsciousness while Mr. Holmes's crimes were potentially being erased by fire, water, and time.

"Police," she rasped, the word barely audible.

The nurse nodded. "They've been waiting to speak with you. I'll let them know you're awake, but the doctor will need to clear you for questioning first."

Emma closed her eyes, exhaustion pulling her back toward darkness. When she next awoke, a doctor was examining her, shining a light into her eyes and listening to her breathing.

"You're a very lucky woman, Ms. Wright," he said. "Another few hours in that storm, with your lungs in that condition, and we might be having a very different conversation."

Lucky. The word seemed obscene given what had happened at Holmes Lodge. Given what had happened to Mark.

By evening, Emma was able to sit up and speak in short sentences, though her voice remained hoarse. When two police officers entered her room, she felt a surge of nervous energy.

"Ms. Wright, I'm Detective Reyes, and this is Detective Morales," the female officer introduced them. "We'd like to ask you some questions about what happened at Holmes Lodge, if you feel up to it."

Emma nodded, gathering her strength. "I need to tell you everything," she whispered.

For the next hour, Emma recounted the nightmare she had lived through. The strange noises, the hidden passages, finding the blueprints, the suitcase in the woods belonging to Jennifer Reeves. Mark's disappearance. The basement with its hooks and surgical tools. The ledger filled with names. The tunnels and her escape through fire.

Throughout her account, the detectives' expressions remained professional, but Emma could see the doubt creeping in as her story grew more horrific.

"So you're saying this man, Mr. Holmes, was... harvesting people for their bones?" Detective Morales asked, his tone carefully neutral.

"Yes," Emma insisted. "He had a ledger with names going back decades. Mark was in it. Jennifer Reeves too, probably."

The detectives exchanged glances. "Ms. Wright," Detective Reyes said gently, "we did recover Jennifer Reeves' backpack from the area last year, but her remains were never found. The assumption was that she was attacked by wildlife."

"Check the ruins," Emma urged. "The basement. There will be evidence."

"We've had teams at the site," Morales said. "The fire destroyed most of the structure, and the heavy rain caused significant flooding in the lower levels. Recovery efforts have been... challenging."

"But you found bodies, right?" Emma pressed, her voice cracking. "The hooks. The tools. They couldn't all have been destroyed."

Another uncomfortable glance between the detectives. "We did recover human remains," Reyes admitted. "Several partial skeletons, badly damaged by fire and water. The medical examiner is working to identify them."

"And Mark?" Emma asked, dreading the answer.

"We found a male body that matches the description of your boyfriend," Morales said carefully. "DNA testing will confirm the identity, but given your statement..."

Emma closed her eyes, tears streaming down her face. She had known, of course, but hearing it confirmed made the loss real in a way it hadn't been before.

"And Mr. Holmes?" she asked after a moment. "Did you find him?"

"No body matching your description of Mr. Holmes has been recovered," Reyes said. "However, the property records show the lodge was owned by a corporation based offshore. We're still tracking down the beneficial owner."

Emma felt a chill that had nothing to do with the hospital's air conditioning. "He could still be alive."

"Ms. Wright," Morales said cautiously, "given the extent of the fire and the collapse you described, it's highly unlikely anyone in those tunnels survived."

"But you haven't found his body," Emma insisted.

The detectives had no answer for that.

In the days that followed, Emma's physical condition improved, but the psychological trauma remained raw. She gave additional statements, reviewed photographs of the ruins, and provided descriptions of both Mr. Holmes and the ledger she had found.

A week after the fire, Detective Reyes returned with an update. "We've confirmed four sets of human remains from the site," she said. "Mark Wright, Jennifer Reeves, and two others from missing persons cases dating back three and seven years."

"Only four?" Emma asked, disbelieving. "There were dozens in that ledger."

"The medical examiner also found a collection of... processed bones," Reyes continued, discomfort evident in her voice. "Over a hundred individual specimens. They appear to have been treated with chemicals and polished."

"His collection," Emma whispered. "He said he was an artist."

"The university's forensic anthropology department is examining them now," Reyes said. "They may be able to identify more victims from these... artifacts."

Emma nodded, a hollow victory. "And Mr. Holmes?"

"Still no sign of him, I'm afraid. We've circulated your description to law enforcement nationwide, but without knowing his real name..."

"He's still out there," Emma said flatly.

Reyes didn't contradict her this time.

Three weeks after the fire, Emma was finally released from the hospital. Her parents had flown in from Arizona, insisting she return home with them to recover. Emma agreed, unable to face returning to the apartment she had shared with Mark.

As she was packing her few belongings, a final visitor arrived—Professor Danvers from the university's anthropology department.

"Ms. Wright," he said, shaking her hand. "I wanted to speak with you before you left. I've been examining the... specimens recovered from Holmes Lodge."

"Have you identified more victims?" Emma asked.

The professor hesitated. "Some, yes. But that's not why I'm here." He lowered his voice. "The bones we received... they're unlike anything I've ever seen. The preservation techniques are extraordinary, almost... artistic."

Emma felt bile rising in her throat. "That's what he called himself. An artist."

"Yes, well..." Danvers cleared his throat uncomfortably. "I wanted you to know that we've pulled all the specimens from circulation. Some of my colleagues wanted to study them, publish papers, but it seemed... disrespectful to the victims."

"Thank you," Emma said simply.

Danvers nodded. "They'll be properly interred once the investigations are complete. I thought you should know."

As he turned to leave, he paused. "One more thing, Ms. Wright. Several of the specimens had... markings. Carvings. Names."

Emma felt her blood run cold. "Was Mark's name there?"

"No," Danvers said. "But yours was."

Chapter 10
Legacy of the Lodge

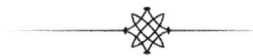

Six months later, Emma sat in her parents' guest room in Phoenix, staring at the blank canvas before her. Since escaping Holmes Lodge, she hadn't been able to paint—every time she picked up a brush, her hands shook uncontrollably.

The therapist she had been seeing called it PTSD. Emma called it survival instinct. Something in her knew that to create art now was to invite Holmes's presence back into her life, to acknowledge the twisted kinship he had tried to establish between them.

"We're both artists, Emma," he had said in the basement. "We see the beauty beneath the surface that others miss."

She shuddered at the memory, setting down her paintbrush untouched. Outside, the Arizona desert stretched beneath a cloudless sky, so different from the misty mountains where Mark had died. Where part of her had died too.

Her phone buzzed with a text from Detective Reyes, who still sent occasional updates:

DNA results back on bone fragments found in tunnel collapse. No match to your description of Holmes. Still working other angles. Stay safe.

Emma wasn't surprised. Part of her had known all along that Mr. Holmes wouldn't be found so easily. He was too careful, too meticulous. A man who had hunted humans for decades wouldn't be careless enough to die in a fire of his own making.

The doorbell rang, pulling her from these dark thoughts. She heard her mother answer it, then call up the stairs: "Emma, honey? There's a package for you."

Emma froze. She never ordered anything to her parents' address. No one knew she was here except the police and her closest friends.

With cautious steps, she descended the stairs. On the entry table sat a small cardboard box, unmarked except for her name and her parents' address written in neat block letters. No return address.

"It was on the porch," her mother explained. "No delivery person or anything."

Emma's hands trembled as she lifted the box. It was lightweight, perhaps the size of a paperback book. Every instinct screamed to throw it away unopened, but she knew she wouldn't find peace until she faced whatever it contained.

In the kitchen, she carefully cut open the tape with a knife. Inside, nestled in crumpled newspaper, was a small object wrapped in velvet cloth. Emma unwrapped it slowly, revealing a polished bone—a human vertebra, gleaming ivory under the kitchen lights.

Her gorge rose as she turned it over. On one side, carved in delicate, flowing script, was her name: *Emma*.

Below it, a single line: *The collection remains incomplete.*

Emma dropped the bone as if it had burned her, stumbling backward against the counter. Her mother rushed in at the sound of her gasping breaths.

"Emma? What's wrong? What is it?"

Unable to speak, Emma pointed at the vertebra on the floor. Her mother picked it up, frowning in confusion. "Is this... some kind of art piece? Why would someone send you this?"

Emma snatched it from her mother's hands. "Call Detective Reyes," she managed to say. "Tell her he found me."

That evening, as police officers dusted the package for fingerprints and questioned neighbors about suspicious vehicles, Emma sat numbly on the couch watching the local news. The anchor's voice barely registered until a familiar image appeared on the screen—a rustic wooden building nestled among pine trees.

"—grand opening this weekend of the newly renovated Stillwater Lodge in northern Colorado," the anchor was saying. "The historic property has been fully restored after changing hands last month. Owner Steven Holloway says he hopes to attract hikers and nature enthusiasts looking for an authentic mountain experience away from the crowds."

The camera cut to a man being interviewed outside the lodge—tall, slender, with silver hair and wire-rimmed glasses. A man whose face Emma knew better than her own after months of nightmares.

The face had been altered subtly—now wearing glasses, a neatly trimmed beard—but the eyes were unmistakable. Cold, assessing, patient.

Mr. Holmes. Alive and starting over with a new name, a new lodge, a new hunting ground.

Emma lunged for her phone, nearly dropping it in her haste to call Detective Reyes. As it rang, her eyes remained fixed on the television, where "Steven Holloway" was smiling at the camera, inviting guests to experience the unique charm of Stillwater Lodge.

"We're quite isolated," he was saying, his cultured voice unchanged. "Perfect for those seeking to... disappear from the world for a while."

As Reyes answered, Emma could only whisper, "He's back. And he's still hunting."

On the screen, Mr. Holmes looked directly into the camera as if he could see her through it, his thin lips curving into the barest suggestion of a smile. The same smile he had worn while explaining his "craft" in the blood-soaked basement of Holmes Lodge.

A chill ran through Emma as she realized the terrible truth: this would never be over. Not until one of them was dead. The bone he had sent wasn't just a threat—it was an invitation. A challenge.

She thought of the carvings on the tunnel walls, the desperate messages left by those who had come before her. The ones who hadn't escaped. Mark's name would be among them now, preserved in bone and memory.

As the news segment ended, Emma squared her shoulders, a cold resolve settling over her. If Mr. Holmes wanted to continue their game of cat and mouse, she would no longer be the hunted.

She had learned from the master himself how to set a trap. And next time, she would make sure the fire consumed him completely.

THE END

Enjoyed this book?

Share your thoughts with a review and help more readers discover it! Your feedback truly makes a difference.

☆ ☆ ☆ ☆ ☆

To be the first to read my next book or for any suggestions about new translations, visit: https://arielsandersbooks.com/

SPECIAL BONUS
Want this Bonus Ebook for *free*?

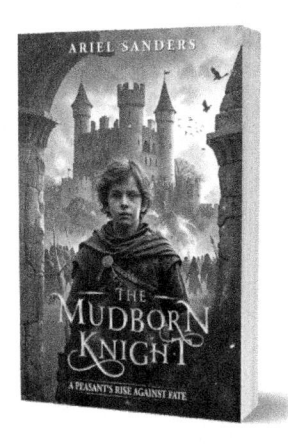

SCAN W/ YOUR CAMERA TO DOWNLOAD THE EBOOK!

Printed in Dunstable, United Kingdom